Joey Goes to Market

by Dottie Makem
illustrated by Dave Sullivan

ISBN 0-15-317207-X – Joey Goes to Market

Ordering Options
ISBN 0-15-318594-5 (Package of 5)
ISBN 0-15-316985-0 (Grade 1 Package)

4 5 6 7 8 9 10 179 02 01

"Wake up!" said Joey's dad.
"It's Saturday. The sky is blue,
and it's warm outside. Let's go
to the market in town."

1

Joey jumped out of bed and ran down to eat. He smiled thinking about going to the market with his dad.

2

"We can buy vegetables
at the market," Dad said to
Joey. "Then we can make
vegetable soup."

"Look at the vegetables!" said Dad. "We can make good soup."

"Wow! Look at all the colors!" Joey said. "I like vegetables with pretty colors!"

4

"Look at these big oranges.
Can we buy some now?" asked
Joey. "I like the color orange.
Let's put them in the soup!"

5

"Yes, we can buy some oranges," answered Dad.

6

"We don't need oranges for vegetable soup," he said. "But let's buy some and make an orange drink."

"How about these green
apples, Dad?" asked Joey.
"Can we buy them? I like the
color green. Let's put them
in the soup!"

8

Dad laughed. "Yes, we can
buy some apples," he said.
"We don't need apples for
vegetable soup, but we can
bake a pie with them."

"How about these red grapes, Dad?" asked Joey. "Can we buy them? I like the color red. Let's put them in the soup!"

10

Dad smiled. "Yes, we can buy some grapes," he said. "We don't need grapes for vegetable soup, but we can make some jam with them."

"We have many pretty colors now!" said Joey.

"Yes," said Dad, "but how can we make vegetable soup? We don't have any vegetables!"

Teacher/Family Member ....

Draw This!
Have your child draw pictures of things Joey got at the market and
tell what Joey and his dad will make with each one.

 School-Home Connection
Invite your child to read Joey Goes to Market to you. Then ask what
your child would buy at the market to make vegetable soup.

Word Count:	253
Vocabulary Words:	blue
	warm
	smiled
	buy
	colors
	orange
Phonic Elements:	Vowel variant: /ou/ow
	town
	down
	wow
	now
	how

....

TAKE-HOME BOOK
Welcome Home
Use with "The Absent-Minded Toad."